D1200898

DATE DUE

9-3-78	OCT 1 0 1997	
7-1-81	SEP 2 0 2002	
3-21-83	SEP 0 9 2003	
10-16-83	JAN 0 5 2004	
2-2	FEB 0 8 2005	
3-10-84	MAR 2 3 2005	
4-12-84	APR 0 6 2005	
10-3-85	MAY 2 4 2006	
2-12-86	DEC 0 6 2006	
10-1-88		
3-16-89	JAN 0 2 2007	
5-3-89	JUL 0 7 2009	
JUN 1 4 1992		
SEP 2 2 1992	MR 2 1 '11	
APR 2 1 1993	SE 2 9 '11	
SEP 1 4 1996	6-11-18	
DEC 2 1 1996 NOV 2 7 1996		

THE
CHALK BOX
STORY

Don Freeman

J.B. Lippincott Company / Philadelphia and New York

To Jeremy and Bambi

U.S. Library of Congress Cataloging in Publication Data
Freeman, Don.   The chalk box story.
SUMMARY: Pieces of colored chalk draw a story about a boy stranded on an island and
the turtle who rescues him.
[1. Colors — Fiction] I. Title.
PZ7.F8747Ch [E]   76-10169   ISBN-0-397-31699-2

This is a chalk box

with eight sticks of chalk

inside waiting to get out.

And this is a piece of paper

       tacked on a board

              waiting to be drawn on.

One day the lid of the box popped open
and all eight sticks of chalk
began to talk at once.

"Let's make a picture," they said.

Blue was the first color to hop out.

"I will draw the sky," said Blue,

"and the ocean too."

This is what Blue drew—

"I am the color of the sun," said Yellow,
"and I am the color of the sand.
I will make a sandy island
in the middle of the ocean
under the hot sun."

This is what Yellow drew—

"I know what I will draw," said Brown,

"a little boy standing on the sandy island

in the middle of the ocean

under the hot sun."

Brown also drew two tree trunks, like this—

"The trees need palm leaves," said Green,

"and there should be a turtle resting

in the sun."

This is what Green drew—

"Why does the boy look so sad?" Purple asked.
"I wonder if he would like something
to play with."

And Purple drew a stick for the boy and made
some designs on
the turtle's shell.

The chalks watched, but the boy did not smile.

"Maybe he wants to go home," said Black.

"I will draw a boat to rescue him."

Off in the distance this is what Black drew—

"The boat is too far away to see the boy,"

White complained.

"I will give him a flag to wave."

And this is what White drew on the end of the stick—

"The boat is still not coming!" Red exclaimed.

"We must do something, quick."

"It's your turn!" cried the other colors.

"Hurry! Hurry!"

Red jumped out of the box and wrote

these two words on the flag—

The chalks peered out of their box and waited,

and waited.

But nothing happened.

"Oh, what a sad picture we've drawn," said Blue.

"And there's nothing we can do

to change it."

Then, all at once,

the turtle lifted her head

and looked up at the little boy

waving the flag.

The boy smiled at the turtle

and climbed onto her back

and together they floated

   out to sea

      all the way

         to the waiting boat.

"Hooray!" shouted the chalks
as the boat sailed away
carrying the boy safely home.

The turtle then returned to her sandy island

in the middle of the ocean

under the setting sun

and went to sleep.

And, ever so slowly,

the eight sticks of chalk

happily closed the lid.

Don Freeman was born in San Diego, California. From the time he was a boy, he wanted to be an artist. In high school he was an accomplished trumpet player, and later, while studying at the Art Students League of New York, he earned his living as a professional musician.

Besides having a great interest in painting and sketching city scenes, Mr. Freeman was an avid theatergoer, which led him to draw his impressions of Broadway plays for the drama pages of such newspapers as the *New York Herald-Tribune* and *The New York Times;* his work has also appeared in *Theater* magazine, *Fortune,* and *The New York Times Magazine.*

Mr. Freeman is the author-illustrator of more than twenty-five books for young readers, as well as numerous books for adults on which he collaborated with other authors. He makes his home in Santa Barbara, California.